Cooties
From Outer Space

By Joan Holub
Illustrated by Jared Lee

Wright Group/McGraw-Hill
19201 120th Avenue NE
Bothell, WA 98011
www.WrightGroup.com

Printed in China through Colorcraft Ltd, Hong Kong

10 9 8 7 6 5 4 3

ISBN: 0-322-04506-1
ISBN: 0-322-04602-5 (6-pack)

Contents

CHAPTER 1
Talking Trash

Don't ever look into the trash cans in your school cafeteria, if you know what's good for you.

For one thing, they can be pretty gross. And for another, you might just find yourself stuck with some unexpected pests. Like I did, a few weeks ago.

When I went to toss out my lunch leftovers, I couldn't help noticing that something in the trash really stunk, even worse than usual. I held my breath and looked inside the trash can. I saw the usual stuff—grape stems, apple cores, mangled plastic wrap.

But mostly, I saw gobs of gloppy Mushroom Surprise, which had been the lunch special that day. I knew from personal experience that it wasn't the Mushroom Surprise that stunk. It didn't really have any smell. Or taste. But strangely enough, it did seem to be wiggling and making weird bubbling sounds. I grabbed a straw and nudged some lumps.

Big mistake.

Shhhhmop! Shmop! Shmop! Three tiny creatures popped up like jack-in-the-boxes. They were each about the size of my plastic Plazmo Action Guys and they were dripping with mushroom goo. Underneath the goo, I could see that one of the creatures was covered with green swirls, one was purple-spotted, and the other was sort of pink plaid. Wild frizzy hair stuck up from their heads like it was electrified.

"Gadbooooque!" shouted the swirly green one. His voice sounded like screechy fingernails on the blackboard. I shivered.

"Www-what do you want?" I asked in a high wobbly voice.

"*Zlixnerp bamboozle slipzog!*"

The pink plaid creature elbowed him and then pointed at his ear.

"*Ixtorp!*" muttered green-swirls. His hand flashed out, bent down his ear, and punched a button behind it. "Sorry. My language translation unit was off," he explained. "What is your label?"

"Label? You m-m-mean name?"

All three creatures nodded.

I shrugged nervously, "G-George D-Dorcas."

They each whipped out thingies that looked like tiny computer books. As they typed, the creatures began arguing.

"Why did you land us in all this goo anyway?" purple-spots was asking.

"I wasn't the one who suggested these landing coordinates if you will remember," said pink-plaid.

"Quiet!" shouted green-swirls. "You will make George Dorcas think that we cannot get along."

Pink-plaid and purple-spots stopped fighting and looked at me with concern. Then they gave me big, fake, salesman smiles, as if they were trying to prove how nice they were.

"Who are you?" I asked, still quivering in my high-tops.

"My label is Hootie," said green-swirls.

"I am Boodie," said purple-spots.

"I am Joody," said pink-plaid.

"We are from planet Cootie," they chorused.

I burst out laughing. I couldn't help it. I mean, I had never seen a real live Cootie before—much less three of them. I didn't even think Cooties really existed.

"This is a joke, right?" I asked.

"No joke," said Hootie.

"Hey, listen. You aren't going to kidnap me or anything, are you?" I asked.

"Get serious," scoffed Hootie. "You are wasting time."

Boodie pointed at my lunch trash. "Do you have toenails in there?"

"Toenails?" I echoed, looking down at my lunch tray. "No! Why would I have toenails in my lunch?"

Joody shoved Boodie aside to glare at me.

"We need toenails!" she insisted.

"What for?" I asked.

"Are you talking to the trash can?" sneered a voice behind me.

I turned around in surprise. At least my top half did. My arms windmilled as I tried to keep my balance.

But it didn't work. I found myself flat on the floor, staring up at Tina Goop and Ed Snidely. "Smooth move, Dorcas," said Ed.

I looked back and forth between them and the trash Cooties. Weren't Tina and Ed even going to mention them?

"Who were you talking to?" asked Tina.

I realized that she and Ed couldn't see the Cooties.

"No one," I said. "I mean—I was just talking to myself."

"First sign of insanity," said Ed, tossing his trash in a high arc. It landed on top of the Cooties. And before Tina, Ed, or the Cooties could say another word, I took off. I didn't stop until I was back in Ms. Blanding's classroom.

CHAPTER 2
Super Stink

Somehow the Cooties managed to track me down. When they found me in Ms. Blanding's class, they greeted me like we were long lost buddies or something.

Hootie hopped onto my shoulder. His head flicked back and forth rapidly as he studied everything in the room with fascination. Ms. Blanding's room had never seemed all that interesting to me—even back at the beginning of the year.

Boodie and Joody began rolling around in Ed Snidely's ratty hair. Ed swatted at them. Boodie hung on, but Joody went flying.

She ended up swinging from the end of Ms. Blanding's nose. I wondered how long she'd be able to hold on.

But I had more important things to worry about. Were the Cooties real? Or was I crazy? If they *were* real, why did they want toenails? Were they planning to roam the earth stealing toenails until every toenail was gone? And after all the toenails were gone, what would they want next? Fingernails? I spread my fingers and tried to imagine them without fingernails. Gross.

Speaking of gross, today in science we were dissecting grasshoppers. The formaldehyde preservative on the bugs really stunk.

But something else stunk worse: Hootie. He absolutely reeked. Like old fish wrapped in dirty gym socks. I decided he must be real. Nothing that smelled this bad could be fake.

Suddenly, Hootie dug his sharp clawlike fingers into my neck. He stuck his face close to mine. "George Dorcas, you must help us," he said.

"W-w-what do you need me for?"

I pulled the front of my shirt up over my nose to shut out some of Hootie's smell. A few other kids had done the same to guard against the formaldehyde fumes, so I didn't look too weird. And this way, no one would see me talking to invisible Cooties.

"We are running out of time," said Hootie desperately.

"Time for what? Is it something about the toenails?" I asked.

"Yes, toenails!" said Hootie. "We must have toenails!"

"What for?" I whispered.

"I have given the Cootie pledge not to reveal our reasons until we have finished our Earth tasks," said Hootie.

Just then I saw Joody stick her head inside Ms. Blanding's nose. Ms. Blanding sneezed. Joody flew across the room, landed on Tina's backpack, and crawled inside.

"Well, are you not the tiniest bit curious?" asked Hootie.

"About the toenails? Well, yeah, but you said—," I began.

"Okay, you forced it out of me," said Hootie. He leaned close to me and whispered, "We need toenails to save your world."

"Huh? Save it from what?" I asked.

"Disgusting creatures with terrible dandruff known on our planet as Copy Cooties. They make copies of every living being they come in contact with. In just days."

Hootie began hopping up and down on my desk waving his arms. I wouldn't have thought it possible, but his smell seemed to grow worse. I tugged my shirt collar tighter over my nose.

"They will clone Earthlings. There will be twenty copies of you in no time, a hundred copies of your friends, a thousand copies of your teacher. Soon no one will know who is real and who is not. Terrible chaos will result —not to mention overpopulation. Eventually it will mean the end of planet Earth and everyone on it."

"And all you need to stop them is toenails?" I asked.

"It will help," said Hootie.

"So—," I began.

"George, do you know?" asked Ms. Blanding.

My nose popped out of my shirt collar. The whole class was staring at me.

"H-huh?" I fumbled.

Ms. Blanding was pointing to a diagram of a grasshopper on the board, but I had no idea what she was asking.

"Eight?" I guessed.

The other kids started giggling. Ms. Blanding frowned.

Suddenly Ralph cried, "A bug's in my ear!"

Ms. Blanding sent him to the nurse for an ear check. But I knew the nurse wouldn't find anything. I had just seen Boodie sail out of Ralph's ear. He somersaulted in midair and landed on my desk, giving me a big grin. Waves of stinky breath whooshed out from between his teeth.

Joody boinged up beside him. She sniffed my grasshopper's leg appreciatively and then sat on it.

Hootie began punching buttons on his computer book.

"What are you writing?" I whispered, ducking my nose back inside my shirt.

"Nothing," said Hootie.

"You are too. I'll bet you're writing that Earthlings are dumb. Don't judge all Earth kids by me. Your whole planet will think we are a bunch of jerks," I said.

"You are no jerk. You will help us defeat the Copy Cooties. You will save your planet. You will be a hero," said Hootie.

I knew I was about as far from a hero as you could get.

"Look, I'm only a kid," I whispered. "I'm not all that smart and I flub up a lot. I don't want it to be my fault if everyone croaks."

"P.U. Something stinks!" Ed announced suddenly, pinching his nose.

Uh-oh.

I kept my head down and tried to look really interested in my bug, hoping Ed wouldn't notice me. He leaned over and sniffed Jay, who sat behind him. Satisfied that it wasn't Jay that stunk, he then sniffed Tina.

Tina gave him a dirty look. I had to get out of here before—

Too late!

Ed leaned toward me. He took a good l-o-o-o-n-g whiff. "Gross! It's Dorky Dorcas," he yelled, holding his nose.

Tina sniffed me. She reared back, fanning a hand in front of her face. "Phew! You do stink! Don't you ever take a bath?"

"It's not me," I said. "It's...," I stopped. I couldn't exactly tell them it was the Cooties.

"Something stinks," complained a kid a few desks away.

"It's George," Tina said. "He has cooties!"

She was just guessing. But as usual, she was right.

I did have Cooties—three of them. They stunk like crazy, and I had to get rid of them!

CHAPTER 3
Here a Cootie

"Why am I the only one who can see you?" I asked the Cooties on the way home. They were riding in pockets of the backpack I had slung over one shoulder.

"We reveal ourselves to aliens on a need-to-know basis," said Hootie.

"Forget all that," said Boodie. "What about the club badge?"

"What club? What badge?" I asked.

"Way to go, Boodie-head," said Joody, giving him a thump. Boodie looked sheepish.

"We cannot tell you all," said Hootie. "But we are members of the Cootie Club.

"We are on a club mission to stop the Copy Cooties from destroying your planet."

"The Cootie Club? Is that like Junior Explorers?" I asked.

"Do Junior Explorers earn badges by completing tasks in a manual?" asked Hootie.

I nodded. In Junior Explorers we had a manual. And we tried to earn badges. So far, I had only earned one. And I had sort of fudged to get that one.

"Then they are the same," said Hootie.

We made it home and up to my room without running into my parents. The Cooties immediately hopped out of my backpack and began poking around my stuff. "How long will it take to nix the Copy Cooties?" I asked.

Hootie looked shifty-eyed, which made me immediately suspicious.

"Not one moment longer than necessary," he said.

"But what do you guess—an hour, a day, a week?" I asked.

"Never mind. When are we ever going to get toenails?" Boodie demanded.

I gulped. "Do you need whole toenails, or just clippings?"

The Cooties huddled up, whispering.

"Clippings will do," Hootie announced at long last.

"You do have toenails, don't you?" Joody asked, sounding concerned.

"Yeah, I've got 'em all right." I giggled, relieved that I wasn't going to have to fight to save my whole toenails. Then I pulled off my sock and wiggled my toes at them.

"This is no laughing matter. We must hurry," said Hootie, with his hands on his hips. I clipped my toenails and gave him some. He tucked them into a small pouch he wore.

"There," I said. "Have a nice trip home."

"Not so fast!" said Hootie. "Toenails are not all we need."

I sighed. "I was afraid of that. What else? Make it quick."

"We must complete a list of tasks in our, uh, Cootie Club manual before the Copy Cooties complete them. That's the only way to stop them from carrying out their evil plan," said Joody. She held up her tiny computer. I saw a ton of scratchy symbols on its screen.

"I can't read it," I said.

"Naturally not," said Joody. "It is written in Cootie. I will read it to you."

"No, let me. You get to do all the fun stuff," whined Boodie.

"It was my idea!" insisted Joody.

"Who is the leader here anyway?" asked Hootie. "I will read it to George Dorcas."

Boodie and Joody quit arguing, but they didn't look happy.

Hootie turned back to me. "Here is the list," he said, and he began reading.

"Number two: Get Earthling toenails. Number three: Learn an Earth game. Number four: Take a photo of planet Cootie from Earth. Number five: Meet the high commander of Earth. Number six: Get an Earthling to guess the Cootie Club password."

"What happened to number one?" I asked, changing into my baseball shirt.

"No time to explain now. We must hurry," warned Hootie. "The Copy Cooties are up to number four."

"How do you know?" I asked.

"We have our ways," said Joody.

"I'll help you get started on all of this weird stuff later," I promised. "But I don't have time right now. I have baseball tonight."

"Do you not care about the future of your planet?" asked Hootie.

"Sure, but I can't miss this game," I told him, tugging on my cap.

"Game? An Earth game?" asked Hootie. "Why did you not say so? That will take care of task number three. Let us go."

"Me first," said Joody, heading for my bedroom door.

"No me!" cried Boodie.

I rolled my eyes. This was going to be the longest day of my life.

"I have a great idea," I told the Cooties on the way to the game. "I think you should let a few more kids see you."

"Are you trying to get rid of us?" asked Hootie.

"Do you not like us?" wailed Boodie, his face crumpling.

"George Dorcas hates us!" sobbed Joody, tears rolling down her cheeks.

"No, no! I like you," I assured them. Boy, were they sensitive. "I just thought you might be able to complete the tasks faster if we get more help."

"Good idea," said Hootie.

"Which Earthlings do you suggest?" asked Boodie.

"I think one of you should hang around with Tina. She makes straight A's." I was sure that would make Tina sound appealing.

"Do you make crooked A's?" asked Boodie.

"What are A's?" asked Hootie.

Oh, brother, I thought.

"I will go with Tina," said Joody.

"Why you?" asked Boodie. "I want to."

"I said it first—," began Joody.

"Enough! Joody goes with Tina," I told Boodie. "You can have Ed. You'll like him better anyway."

Boodie nodded reluctantly.

That'll fix Tina and Ed, I thought. If I could only figure out a way to ditch Hootie, things would be just about perfect. But I couldn't—without hurting his feelings. At least one Cootie was bound to be better than three.

We reached the ballpark with ten minutes to spare. I dropped by the other team's dugout, pretending to wish them luck.

"Good luck!" I called to Tina, as Joody backflipped from my shoulder to hers. Tina scrunched her face at me.

"Hit a homer," I told Ed, as Boodie vaulted from my baseball cap to his.

Ed glared at me suspiciously. "Don't worry, I will."

A few hours later, my team won—no thanks to me. I struck out both times I was at bat. What else was new? I should have been used to it by now, but I was kind of embarrassed to strike out in front of the Cooties. They would think I was a real loser.

"Wow, you were fantastic!" said Hootie on the way home after the game.

"What do you mean? I struck out both times I was at bat," I said.

"Yes, it must have been difficult to dodge the flying orb with your bat-stick," said Hootie, with admiration. "None of the others performed so well as you."

"But...," I began. Wait a minute—if I told him he'd misunderstood, it would only delay things. Who would it hurt if he learned the game wrong?

CHAPTER 4
There a Cootie

The next day I felt really crabby. It had taken forever to get to sleep thanks to Hootie. He had some very annoying habits.

First of all, he hummed off key.

As soon as I got him to stop humming, he started drumming his claw fingers. It was like water torture.

When I asked him to stop that, he began sighing over and over again. Next it was burping. Then lip smacking. He kept me awake half the night.

I perked up once I got to school and saw Tina and Ed. They were standing close together, whispering. And they looked as tired as I felt. Joody and Boodie waved to Hootie and me from the pockets of Tina and Ed's backpacks.

"Hey, Tina, what's that new perfume you're wearing?" a kid called as he walked by her. "Eau de skunk?"

Tina's face turned redder and redder until she looked ready to explode.

At lunch, Ed and Tina cornered me by the cafeteria door.

"Will you Cooties excuse us for a minute?" Tina asked. She set Joody on the garbage bin. Ed grabbed Hootie and Boodie and set them down, too.

We moved a few feet away, leaving the Cooties happily scouting through the trash.

"Did you sic those Cooties on us?" Tina demanded.

"Maybe," I said, shrugging. I couldn't help grinning though.

"You did!" shouted Ed.

"What did we ever do to you?" Tina asked.

"Where do I begin?" I asked. "First there was that lovely nickname—Dorky. And then there was the time you told Marnie Droodle I liked her. Then there was the time—"

"Okay, okay, so we haven't been best friends. We didn't think you were mad about that stuff," said Ed.

"If we say we're sorry, will you take the Cooties back?" asked Tina.

I shook my head.

"But they stink!" she protested.

"Yeah, I know," I said.

Ed looked over to be sure the Cooties weren't listening. "Did they tell you about saving the planet from the Copy Cooties?"

"Yeah," I said.

We both looked at Tina. "They told me, too," she said in disgust. "It was supposed to be some big secret. *Hah!* Those Cooties are a bunch of blabbermouths."

"Look," I told Tina and Ed, "the sooner we help them, the sooner they'll leave."

"What do you mean 'WE'?" said Ed. "This is your mess—"

"Uh-oh. Here comes trouble," Tina interrupted.

I turned to see Ronald, Peter, and Sam, three of the biggest bullies in school, coming straight for us.

"Great, a bully encounter. Just what I needed to make this week perfect," I groaned.

Suddenly Hootie made a flying leap for my pants leg. He scrambled up to my shoulder like a monkey climbing a tree.

"Run!" shouted Hootie. "It is Rudey, Pootie, and Snooty!"

"Who?" I asked in surprise.

"The Copy Cooties! Run for your lives!" shouted Hootie.

"What do you mean? It's just Ronald, Pete, and Sam," Tina said.

"No! They are possessed by Copy Cooties!" shrieked Joody.

"Did you not notice all that dandruff? It is the Copy Cooties' skin flakes. They shed like crazy!" yelled Boodie.

It did look like the bullies were leaving a trail of snow behind them. Better safe than sorry. Tina, Ed, and I took off running.

"You can run, but you can't hide!" shouted Sam.

We managed to dodge the bullies and their Copy Cootie hitchhikers by hiding out in the library. Sitting around a table, we had to sneak bites of our lunches whenever Mr. Pickie, the librarian, wasn't looking.

"What'll the Copy Cooties do to us if they catch us?" I asked the Cooties.

"Whatever is necessary to stop you from helping us," said Hootie.

"Does that include killing us?" Ed asked.

"Of course not. Freezing you, maybe," said Hootie.

"But just long enough for them to take over your world," added Joody.

Ed, Tina, and I shared horrified looks.

"Well, uh, let's get down to business then. What's left on the task list?" I asked.

"Number four is 'Take a photo of planet Cootie from Earth,'" said Boodie.

"Does anybody have a camera?" asked Tina, looking from Ed to me.

"I do, but it's not telescopic," said Ed. "And I doubt the flash works a zillion miles from here."

"Our beloved planet Cootie is only 49,000,000 miles away from our present location," said Joody.

I grabbed a book on stars and planets from a library shelf to try and figure out exactly where Cootie was. As I set it on our table, it fell open to a page of planet photos.

"There it is!" shouted Boodie. "There's Cootie!" He dashed across the page to run his claw fingers lovingly over one of the planets.

It was the red one right next to Earth.

"That's the planet Cootie?" I asked in disbelief.

Tina turned the book so she could see. "That's not Cootie. It's Mars!"

"You mean Cooties are really Martians?" asked Ed.

"No, we are Cooties. It is our planet and we named it 'Cootie.' You Earthlings have a lot of nerve naming our planet without asking us. How would you like it if we named your planet for you?" asked Hootie.

"He's got a point," said Tina.

Rip! I turned just in time to see Boodie and Joody carefully tear the photo of Mars from the book.

"What are you doing?" I demanded in horror.

"This photo of Cootie was taken from Earth," said Joody. "We will use it to fulfill task number four."

"But I thought you had to take the photo yourself," said Tina.

"So we bend the rules a little. Who will know?" asked Boodie.

Hootie nodded. "Boodie is right. It is good enough," he said.

Talk about fudging! Tina, Ed, and I looked at each other in exasperation.

"Okay, on to number five," I said, deciding not to give the Cooties a chance to change their minds. "What was it again?"

"It—" began Joody.

"My turn! My turn!" said Boodie, hopping up and down frantically.

Joody huffed, but gave in.

"Number five," read Boodie. "Meet the high commander of Earth."

The bell rang and Hootie sighed as we all jumped up. "Another interruption. I guess this means back to class." Mr. Pickie scowled suspiciously at us as we filed out.

"Number five is going to be tough," said Tina on the way to class.

"Why?" asked Joody.

"Because there is no high commander of our entire planet for you to meet. No one tells everyone on Earth what to do," I explained.

"But who makes the rules here?" asked Boodie, gesturing around the hall.

"Here at school? The principal," I said.

"Then take us to see the principal," said Hootie. "That will be good enough."

"You can't go to see the principal for no reason," I protested. "You have to get into trouble first."

"Well, it looks like we're about to," warned Ed, as we approached our class.

I glanced up to see Mr. Pickie standing beside Ms. Blanding at the classroom door. He was gesturing wildly at something he held.

Oh no! It was the planet book. He must have discovered that a page was missing!

Ms. Blanding asked, "George? Tina? Ed? Did one of you tear a page out of this book?"

Tina, Ed, and I looked at the Cooties and then at each other. There was no way we could tell the truth without sounding bonkers.

"Yeah, I guess so," I said.

"I knew they were up to something!" said Mr. Pickie. "And I found crumbs in their chairs, so they were eating in the library as well!"

Ms. Blanding sighed. "I guess we'll just have to see what Mr. Hardhart has to say about this."

CHAPTER 5
Cootie Lies

"I understand from Ms. Blanding that you have been destroying school property and eating in the library," said Mr. Hardhart. His beady eyes drilled holes in Ed, Tina, and me.

We knew one of us should say something, but none of us had the guts.

Hootie, Boodie, and Joody leaped down from our shoulders and planted themselves on Mr. Hardhart's desk. Mr. Hardhart wrinkled his nose and sniffed.

"Books are in the library for all students to enjoy," he continued. Hootie leaped onto Mr. Hardhart's long nose.

Mr. Hardhart's eyes began watering, like they do when you smell onions. He gave Tina, Ed, and me a weird look.

Hootie hung on for dear life as Mr. Hardhart hurried across the room to open the window.

"We're sorry—" began Tina.

"Yes, yes. That's okay. You may go now," said Mr. Hardhart, coming back to his desk.

We looked at him in surprise.

"That's it?" squeaked Ed.

The principal was holding a handkerchief to his nose now.

"Yes! Now go!" he boomed.

Hootie scampered down his necktie. The three Cooties leaped back on our shoulders and we all jumped up and zoomed out of the principal's office.

"Oh, I almost forgot," Mr. Hardhart called after us, poking his head out of his door. "You'll have to pay for the book. That'll be $7.95 from each of you. And no more eating in the library."

We nodded.

I took a step toward him to test my theory that he was afraid of our smell.

"Uh, yes, that'll be all," he said, shutting his door in my face. I was right!

"We got off pretty easy," said Ed, suddenly cheerful.

"Yeah," I said. "Sometimes it pays to be stinky." Tina, Ed, and I laughed.

"Well at least that takes care of task number five," said Tina. "What's left?"

"Just one task more," said Hootie. "And that is to get you Earthlings to say the Cootie Club password." He looked at us as though that might take some doing.

"The Copy Cooties are on the last task, too. We must hurry!" said Boodie.

"Why don't you just tell us the password?" I suggested.

"No! You must guess it!" said Joody.

"Can't you fudge a little? Who'll know?" I prodded.

Hootie shook his head. "This is one task that must be completed properly. You must earn the privilege of learning the password."

"How about a hint?" asked Tina.

"It rhymes with *Cootie*," said Boodie.

"Big surprise," I grumbled.

"Little word? Big word?" Tina asked.

"What is this—charades?" Ed asked.

"Medium-sized," said Boodie.

"Let's go through the alphabet," Tina suggested to Ed and me. "We're bound to hit on it eventually."

"*Achoodie, babbalootie, capootie, . . .*" We went from A to Z until we found ourselves giggling, "*...Yodelootie, zappadoodie!*"

"Close, but no cigar," said Boodie.

"Which one was the closest?" Ed asked.

"Next to last," said Boodie.

Joody thumped him in annoyance.

"You are giving too many hints."

"Am not!" said Boodie.

While they argued, Ed, Tina, and I began testing out every possible *Y* word we could come up with that rhymed with *Cootie*. We must have run through a hundred when suddenly—

"That is it!" the three Cooties shouted.

"Which one?" I asked.

"Yahootie," they all three cried. They leaped into the air, slapping the bottoms of their feet together.

"We have done it!" shouted Hootie.

"We have completed all of the tasks!" shouted Joody.

"We have won the game!" shouted Boodie.

"Game?" I echoed.

Boodie slapped a hand over his mouth as though to recall his words. Hootie and Joody scowled at him.

"You mean this was all just some dumb game?" I asked.

"Not dumb. It is the Cootie Club Dibs Game," said Hootie. "To win the Earth Badge, you have to be the first team to complete the tasks. Then you get dibs on Earth. It works the same on every planet."

"Was there ever really any danger from the Copy Cooties?" asked Tina.

"No. They are dandruffy pests, but they do not really replicate. They are called Copies because they want to be just like us."

"But why make up all that end of the world stuff?" I asked. "Why not just tell us it was a game?"

"Task number one was to secure the help of Earthlings by telling them a fib," explained Hootie. "We are disqualified if we tell our true purpose before the tasks have all been completed."

"I can't believe you got us in trouble with the school bullies, the principal, and our teacher—all for a game," said Ed.

"You do not like us!" cried Joody.

"You hate us!" wailed Boodie.

"No, we're just mad," said Tina. "You've caused a lot of trouble for us."

"Do not worry," said Hootie. "We will fix everything before we depart."

"NO!" I shouted. "You've done enough."

Hootie shrugged. "Okay, but the Copy Cooties are still around. They are very competitive and will not be happy that you helped us win. But if you wish us to leave, we will. Good-bye."

"Bye," chorused Boodie and Joody.

They snapped their little claw fingers and disappeared as quickly as you could say *Shhhhmop! Shmop! Shmop!*

Tina, Ed, and I stared at the empty space where the three Cooties had been and then at each other.

"They're gone," I said in amazement.

"Thanks a lot, Dorcas," said Ed. "Now we'll be at the mercy of the Copy Cooties."

"Uh-oh," said Tina. "Here they come!"

CHAPTER 6

The Copies Are Coming!
The Copies Are Coming!

Rudey, Pootie, and Snooty came riding along on their bullies, Ronald, Pete, and Sam. They soon surrounded us.

"George Dorcas. Tina Goop. Ed Snidely. You are guilty of helping the Cooties get the Earth Badge," said Rudey.

"Sorry," I said spreading my hands.

"Sorry is no good," said Pootie. "You must be punished."

Suddenly, the Copy Cooties began shedding. It was a dandruff blizzard. We were all coughing and choking.

Then I heard a familiar sound. *Shhhhmop! Shmop! Shmop!* When the snowstorm cleared, Hootie, Joody, and Boodie stood between the Copy Cooties and us.

"Boy, am I ever glad you came back," I croaked.

"We never left," said Hootie. "We merely became temporarily invisible."

"We knew the Copies would be out for revenge when they learned that you helped us," said Joody.

"You did not really think we would leave you in the lurch, did you?" asked Boodie.

"We have dibs on George Dorcas and his planet," Hootie told the Copy Cooties. "Now scram."

Without a word, the scowling Copy Cooties disappeared. *Snnnick! Snick! Snick!*

"Where'd they go?" asked Ed.

"On to the next game on planet Snitt," said Boodie.

"Where'd who go?" Ronald asked. The bullies didn't seem to remember the Copy Cooties or to see the Cooties anymore.

"Uh—nobody," I said.

"Are you making fun of us, Dorcas?" said Pete.

"No, he's not," said Ed.

"Buzz off," said Tina.

"Yeah! Buzz oooooofffff!" echoed Hootie, Boodie, and Joody.

Waves of stinky Cootie breath zoomed toward the bullies. Their eyes watered. Their noses scrunched up.

"Gross! You guys stink!" they shouted. They brushed by us and took off.

"We must go," announced Hootie. "The Copies have already started on Snitt."

"What if they come back?" Ed asked.

"We have dibs on Earth now. They have to stay away," said Joody.

Hootie patted his pouch as though he was making sure he wasn't forgetting anything. "Now I guess this is really good-bye."

"We would like to stay longer...," began Joody.

"...But we must hurry to planet Snitt," finished Boodie.

The Cooties seemed worried that they would offend us by leaving. But we weren't about to try to stop them.

"Have a good trip," I said, giving them a little wave.

Shhhhmop! Shmop! Shmop! And just like that, we were 100 percent Cootie-free.

All through science that afternoon, I kept thinking about the Cooties. Then Ms. Blanding called on me. "George, can you tell us the name of this planet?"

I looked up. She was pointing at the fourth planet from the sun. "Cootie," I said. The whole class laughed. "I mean Mars," I said sheepishly. I looked over at Tina and Ed. We shared a secret smile.

From then on, the three of us did a lot of stuff together. And do you think we ever miss the pitter-patter of little Cootie claws? Are you kidding?

I mean, let's face it, who wants Cooties?